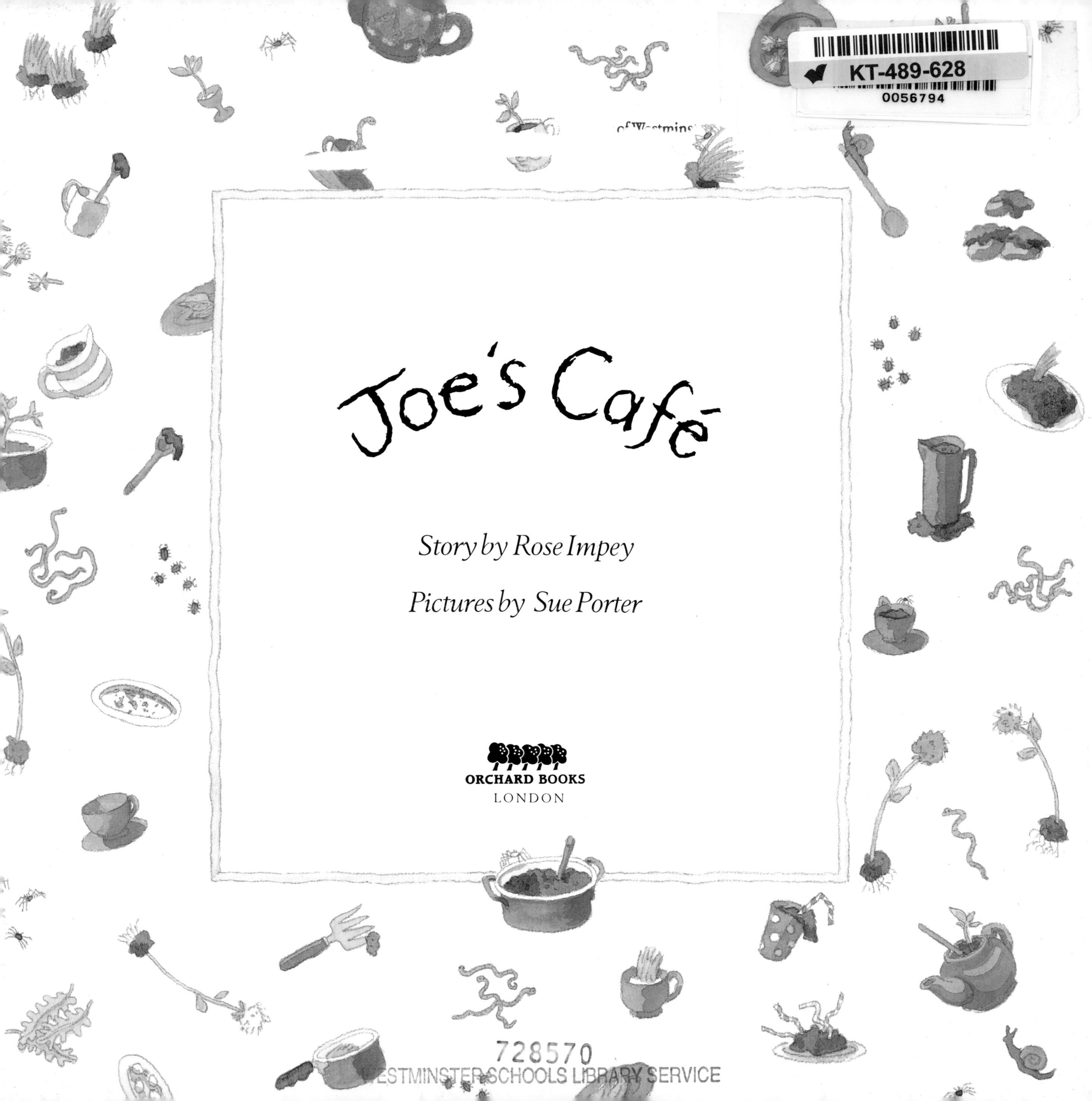

Joe's Café

Story by Rose Impey

Pictures by Sue Porter

ORCHARD BOOKS
LONDON

For my brother Graham,
who got lost

ORCHARD BOOKS
96 Leonard Street, London EC2A 4RH
Orchard Books Australia
14 Mars Road, Lane Cove, NSW 2066

Designed by Sue Porter for Orchard Books
First published in Great Britain 1990
First paperback publication 1991
This edition published 1993
A CIP catalogue record for this book is available from the British Library.
1 85213 227 2 (hardback)
1 85213 563 8 (paperback)
Printed in Hong Kong

It was a hot sunny day and Mum was busy baking. She said to Joe, "Take Amy out in the garden for me, there's a good boy. I shan't be long." She put on Amy's sun hat. "Now, remember," she said, "Joe's in charge."

Joe groaned. He did love his little sister, but the trouble was Amy was too small to play any of Joe's games.

She couldn't play at pirates on the climbing frame. She kept on falling into the sea.

"Watch out! The sharks'll get you," Joe told her. But Amy didn't know about sharks.

She couldn't play at hospitals. She wouldn't lie down and pretend to be ill. Amy spent too much time lying down in real life.

She was more interested in how Dad's bike worked.

"Oh, Amy! Look at you," said Joe.

And she couldn't play Joe's favourite game either — Creepy Crawly Café.

"You mustn't *really* eat them," said Joe. "Just pretend."

In fact, the only game Amy liked to play was hide and seek. She loved secret places where she could sit, sucking her thumb, hiding, until Joe came to find her.

She hid in all sorts of places:

behind the wheelbarrow,

in the flowerbed,

under Mum's washing.

When Joe found her he said,
"Oh, there you are."

"Boo!" said Amy, and she laughed as if it was a real game. Then the minute Joe turned his back, off she went again.

Joe began to feel hot and bad-tempered. He didn't want to spend the afternoon searching for Amy.

"You're a nuisance and I'm fed up with you," he told her.

After that Joe went back to his café and Amy had to wait a very long time to be found.

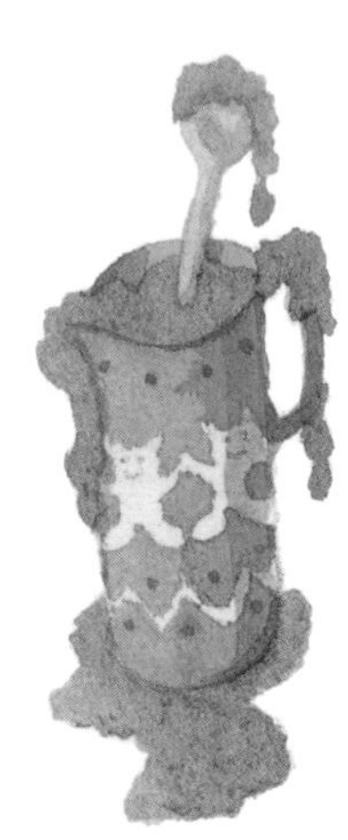

Dad had dug a hole at the end of the lawn to make a sandpit for them. It wasn't finished yet so there was no sand, but Joe had smoothed out a comfy place for his bottom where the soil was soft and easy to dig. He made a hole, poured in the water and stirred it with an old wooden spoon. He loved it when the mud went slip, slop, slurp.

On the menu in Joe's café were lots of interesting dishes:

Joe's Café

worm pies and caterpillar Cakes

Mud flavoured Milk Shakes

sloppy Spider stew

slug sandwhiches

And, of course, plenty of plain mud pies.

Sometimes Joe carried his mud pies to the front gate to see if there were any customers passing by.

Today it was very quiet in the lane but soon he saw Mrs Griffiths, who lived at the farm, walking home from the bus.

"Would you like to come to my café?" Joe called to her.

"I was just thinking about a cup of coffee," said Mrs Griffiths, "and perhaps a little cake."

"I've got some delicious Snail Buns," said Joe.

"My favourite," said Mrs Griffiths.

He handed her a bucket and a plastic plate. And then Joe passed lots of other things for her to try, until all his dishes were lined up outside in the lane.

"Mmmm, I feel much better for that," said Mrs Griffiths. "How much do I owe you?"

"Errm, ten pence," said Joe.

"What a cheap café," she said. "I shall come here again." She gave Joe a new *twenty* pence piece. "You can keep the change."
Then she smiled and waved goodbye.

Joe kept opening his fist and looking at the money shining in the sun. Quickly he opened the gate to collect his dishes, to take them back to his café, so that he could make some more food to sell.

While Joe had been busy selling tea and buns, Amy had found a new secret place to hide — right in the middle of the lilac bush. It was cool and cosy, with the smell of lilac around her. She waited for ages, crushing the lilac flowers between her fingers.

But this time Joe never came. He had completely forgotten about Amy; he had forgotten he was in charge. And now because he was excited — and because his hands were full — Joe forgot another very important thing: to close the front gate. Leaving it wide open, he walked back along the path, sat down in the soil and started to dig.

When Amy finally came out of her hiding place
she saw Joe with his back to her, still busy
with his café. So Amy thought she would
do some digging of her own. She found
a spade on the path and dug it into
the flowerbed. Up popped one
of Mum's flowers and fell
down on the ground.

Amy laughed. "All fall down," she said. She dug up another one, that lay on its side too. And a few more along the path until she came to the front gate. When she saw it wide open Amy smiled. And then, because she was just a baby and there was no one to stop her, Amy kept on walking, out into the lane, dragging the spade behind her. Off she went, wearing only a nappy.

It was quite some time before Joe missed her. He suddenly noticed how quiet it was. He looked for her in all the usual places:

under the wheelbarrow,

in the flowerbeds,

behind the dustbin,

under the washing.

But Amy was nowhere to be seen.

Soon Joe noticed Mum's flowers lying on the soil. He followed the trail to the front gate — *which was still wide open.* Then Joe knew what had happened and, what's more, Joe knew it was his fault.

He stepped out into the lane. It was quiet and still. The sun beat onto the road and onto Joe's head. He looked up the lane which led to the main road. He hoped Amy hadn't gone that way.

He looked down the lane which led to the farm. Perhaps she had gone that way. But how could he know? There was no one to ask. Joe didn't know what to do next.

He knew what he should have done. He should have run straight into the house and told Mum. But Joe didn't do that because he had been left in charge. He desperately wanted to find Amy, before Mum realised she was gone.

Joe wasn't allowed out in the lane, but he ran quickly to the first house. He went up the path and knocked hard on the door.

No one came. The house was silent and empty. Joe tried the next one and the next, but they too seemed to stare at him, without answering. By the time Joe reached the last house he was feeling scared. He'd never been this far — all on his own.

At last someone did answer.
Mr Garner opened his door, rubbing his eyes.
"Have you seen Amy?" Joe asked him. "I've lost her."
But Mr Garner had been having a nap;
he hadn't seen anyone.
"Does your mum know she's gone?"
Joe shook his head; his eyes filled with tears.
"I was supposed to be in charge."
"Don't worry," said Mr Garner, "she can't
have gone far on those little legs. You wait,
while I put my shoes on, then I'll help
you find her."

Joe sat on a stone by the gate at the end of the lane. The tears ran down his face. He felt someone's hot breath on him. It was Bella, Mr Garner's dog. Joe stroked her and rested his head against hers.

"I've lost Amy," he whispered, as if the dog might be able to tell him where to look. But Bella just panted and wagged her tail.
Joe had never felt more unhappy in his life.

Then, through his tears, he saw Bella slip under the gate. She began to bark. Joe climbed up onto the gate to see why. In the distance someone was waving. It was Mrs Griffiths and by the hand she was leading a small figure, wearing only a nappy.

"Mr Garner!" Joe called. "I've found her!"

He climbed over the gate and ran as fast as he could to meet them. When he reached Amy he hugged her and squeezed her until she could hardly breathe.

"I do love you," he whispered. "And you're not a nuisance."

But Amy waved him away with a sticky hand, clutching a large chocolate biscuit. "Wait till Mum sees your face," said Joe. There was chocolate all over it.

Joe pulled up Amy's nappy, which by now was almost round her knees, and took her other hand.

He would have liked to carry Amy but after her adventure Amy felt far too grown up for that.

They said goodbye to Mrs Griffiths, then Joe and Amy walked slowly back along the track to where Joe could see Mum waiting with Mr Garner by the gate. He knew what she would say. "Oh, Joe, how could you?"

The tears came at once. "I'm really sorry," he said. And Mum could see he was. She felt too relieved to be angry. She gave him a hug.

"What we need now," she said, "is a cup of tea."

"You could come to my café," said Joe. "I'll make you a nice cup of Beetle Tea."

Mum smiled. "Why don't you come to my café instead?" she said. "I've finished all that baking."

And since it was such a beautiful, sunny day Joe said, "We could have a picnic, in the garden. Just you and me... and Amy."